The Mysterious Misadventures of

FOY RIN JIN

A Decidedly Dysfunctional Dragon

by Jim Friedman   pictures by Patti Stren

HarperCollinsPublishers

The Mysterious Misadventures of Foy Rin Jin: A Decidedly Dysfunctional Dragon

Library of Congress Cataloging-in-Publication Data
Friedman, Jim, date
  The mysterious misadventures of Foy Rin Jin: A decidedly dysfunctional dragon / by Jim Friedman ;
pictures by Patti Stren.
      p.   cm.
  Summary: A young dragon breathes water instead of fire and saves a burning house.
  ISBN 0-06-028000-X. — ISBN 0-06-028551-6 (lib. bdg.)
  [1. Dragons—Fiction.   2. Fire extinction—Fiction.]   I. Stren, Patti, ill.   II. Title.
PZ7.F8977Me   1999   98-12140
[E]—dc21   CIP
                                                                                          AC

1 2 3 4 5 6 7 8 9 10
❖
First Edition

for shel, my shepherd

5/10/99

This book is dedicated to

Big Dan, Little Josh, Jazzy Jenny,

Airy Ashley, Heavenly Helena,

Maximum Max, Clara, the Scorp

AND

Alice, the Face.

—J.F.

To my big brother, David,

'cause he's the greatest at everything;

to Cara Zacks, Daniel Zacks,

Rebecca Cherniak, Aaron Cherniak,

Annemarie Gerber, Lukas Gerber,

Liam McNally, Stephen McNally,

John Cirigliano, and Gary Senick

because I adore all of you, and, of course,

to my darling husband Richard,

with love.

—P.S.

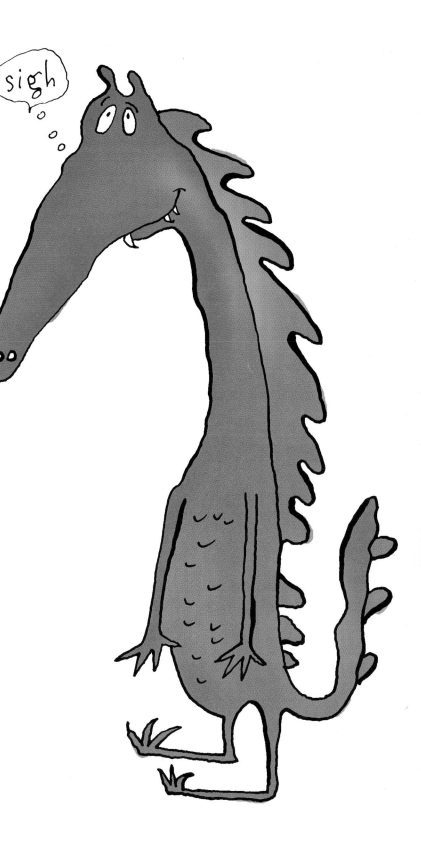

Flame Day was a most special day on the icy white slopes of Skytop Mountain. It was the one day of the year on which the young dragons of Dragon Plateau were initiated into the ancient secret art of fire-breathing.

This year, everyone was especially excited, because among the group of youngsters would be Foy Rin Jin, the biggest, handsomest, reddest, shiniest, nicest young dragon in anyone's memory. Everyone thought that Foy Rin Jin's would be the most unforgettable fire-breathing performance ever. And polite, modest, and agreeable Foy Rin Jin thought so, too.

The great day came.

First, the Grand Elder retold the old legend about the young dragon who discovered fire-breathing by accident when he did something in his throat that made him breathe fire. It gave him quite a shock and several blistered toes. But this clever fellow realized how useful it could be in cooking, although it was also dangerous. And that's why young dragons don't learn the secret throat trick till Flame Day.

Then the Grand Elder proclaimed:

"Let the ceremonies begin!"

To each young, hopeful dragon in turn he whispered the fire-breathing secret. Each nodded, inhaled—and blew all sorts of fire, from great bursts of flame to little hiccupy flickers and sparks.

Finally, only Foy Rin Jin was left. All eyes were upon him. The Grand Elder stood on tiptoe and whispered in his ear. Foy Rin Jin nodded, smiled, and sucked in huge amounts of air. Then, with a mighty roar, he blew out . . .

yikes

Whooooops

aaaargh!

. . . nothing.

There was a stunned silence.

He tried again.

Nothing. Just a puff of air.

Groans rippled through the crowd.

To give him encouragement, the Grand Elder asked everyone to form a big circle around Foy Rin Jin. At his signal, every dragon blazed forth while Foy Rin Jin began turning faster and faster as he inhaled until, spinning furiously, he rose seven feet into the air. And—with a sky-splitting bellow—he let loose an unbelievable blast of . . .

Water!

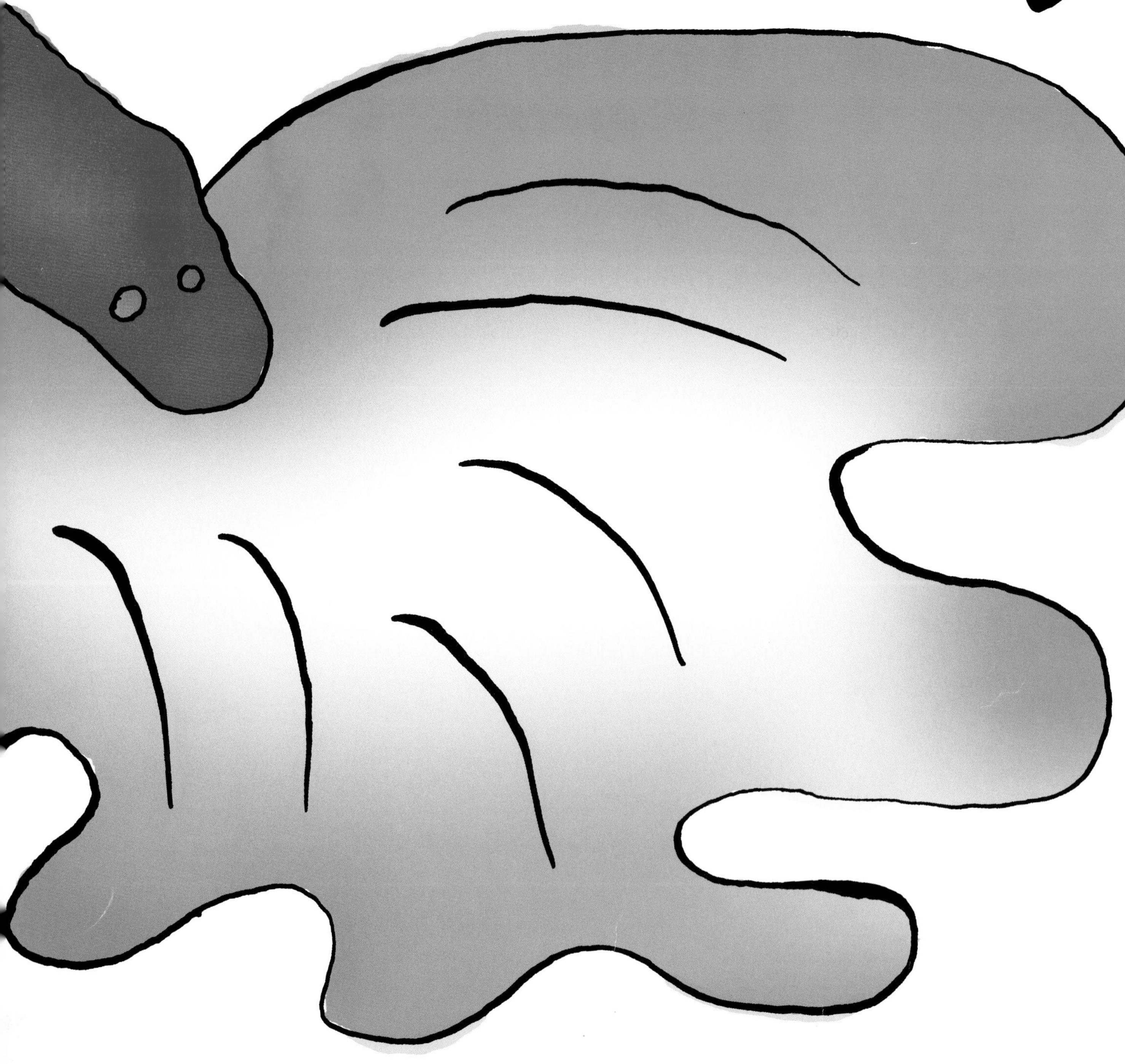

Torrents, floods, maelstroms spewed higgledy-piggledy in every which-what direction. Every dragon's fire was instantly snuffed out. Enormous clouds of steam hissed heavenward, turned into icicles, and clattered down on the tails and scales of three hundred fifty-five drenched and punctured dragons, who scrambled madly in the sudden blackness to escape the shower of icy daggers.

Foy Rin Jin's performance was, indeed, unforgettable. Fortunately, no one was seriously hurt.

As the morning star climbed high in the eastern sky, a bedraggled and bewildered Foy Rin Jin limped sadly home, slunk into his cave, and, passing the thirty-one relatives who groaned and licked wounds in their sleep, curled up in a dark corner and sighed, "I'm a complete failure, a washout."

Woe is me

The next day, everybody acted as if nothing had happened. The only unusual thing was Foy Rin Jin's breakfast. His mother made him a large bowl of chili peppers with garlic and hot sauce. She said, "This will put some fire in your belly." Foy Rin Jin preferred oatmeal, but he bravely swallowed every bit, even though the heat brought tears to his eyes. His mother kissed him and shoved him outside to "go practice." He found a lonely spot up on the mountain and practiced.

The breakfast *did* put fire in his belly. It produced enough boiling water to melt a large patch of ice and cause a snowslide that almost buried Dragon Plateau.

icicle cream pie

yum

Again, not a word was said. Everyone remained just as nice as icicle cream pie, his favorite dessert, which made Foy Rin Jin feel worse than ever.

That night, while everyone was asleep, Foy Rin Jin made a painful decision. He would run away from home. Right now, before he weakened and changed his mind.

Foy Rin Jin tiptoed out of his room, tears streaming down his cheeks. He stooped down to kiss his sleeping mother, who stirred as a tear fell onto her face but didn't waken. At the mouth of the cave, he turned briefly for one last look, then squared his shoulders bravely and headed for LowLow Flateau.

Bye-bye Mummy

Dragons *never* went to LowLow Flateau.

They knew almost nothing about the place except that it was down, down, down, that it was very hot, green, flat, and yucky, and that it was inhabited by creatures called *peoples* who, Foy Rin Jin had heard, were strange, rude, and mean.

Foy Rin Jin knew what *strange* meant. *Strange* was what had happened to him on Flame Day. And *rude* meant someone who interrupted when you were speaking. But what did *mean* mean? Well, whatever *mean* meant, it couldn't be any worse than the kindness that had made him feel so bad.

He trudged down the mountain.

By morning, Foy Rin Jin knew he was in LowLow Flateau. It was very hot and flat and green and yucky.

And standing in his path was an odd-looking creature. It stood still on one thick brown leg, out of which grew many crooked arms and fingers covered with thousands of little green scales and lots of round red things. Was this a *peoples*?

whoa

Ditto

Foy Rin Jin stepped up to the creature and politely said, "Pardon me, sir or madam. My name is Foy Rin Jin. I am a young dragon, and this is my first visit to LowLow Flateau. I wonder if you would kindly give me directions, as I am unfamiliar with the customs of your country."

The creature ignored him.

Strange, surely, and rude, maybe, but was it mean? It was difficult to tell since the creature didn't seem to have eyes, ears, or a mouth. Foy Rin Jin began to introduce himself again when one of the round red things fell—*kerplop!*—right into his mouth. He was so surprised, his jaws clamped shut, crushing it.

"Good grief!" he cried. "What have I done?"

What you have done, answered his stomach, is eat a delicious round red thing. And since it's way past breakfast time, why don't you have another?

Good idea, Foy Rin Jin agreed, and politely asked if he could have one more.

Again, there was no reply, so he ate one more. And then another. The little green scales were tasty, too.

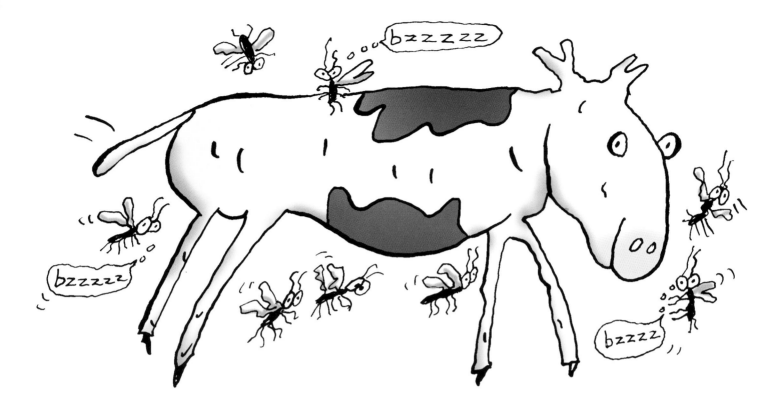

Later, as he lay contentedly picking his teeth with the remains of the leg—it was somewhat tough, but all right—Foy Rin Jin noticed another creature nearby. It was acceptable-looking, but its legs were too long and skinny, its tail was pitiful, and it had two long, curved teeth sticking out of its forehead. Its eyes were half-closed, and it kept chewing on something, which made Foy Rin Jin think that it might be a bit dull. He introduced himself anyway. After a long pause, the creature said, "Mmmmuuuhh!" turned, and slowly wandered off, its silly tail swishing back and forth at some little black buzzy things that flew around it.

Hmmm . . . wonder if it's a . . . no, not likely. . . .

Foy Rin Jin liked the feel of the soft green stuff he was lying on. *Maybe I'll rest a bit,* he thought, and he began to snore.

Hey wake up

Whoa

I vote we go home

WAKE UP!

Open your eyes now!

Run!

Hey, pal

Rise and shine

In his dream, he heard a high-pitched shout that sounded like "Uncle Foon! Uncle Foon! My abbletry! It's gone!" (*Abbeltry? What is abbeltry?* wondered Foy Rin Jin)—and another, scratchy voice, farther away, saying, "Don't be silly, Nephew Chung. An apple tree doesn't disappear. Now, where are my spectacles?" (*Oh, appeltry. What's appeltry?*) Foy Rin Jin opened his eyes. "Yaaah!" A creature stood near him, loudly chirping, "Yaaah!! Yaaah!!!" its eyes and mouth widening with each yaaah. Then it fled down a hillside, yaaahing all the while. Foy Rin Jin decided it must be some sort of unfortunate bird, for though it flapped its wings as it ran, it never quite got off the ground.

Why is it trying to frighten me? Foy Rin Jin wondered.

At the bottom of the hill, the bird crashed into another bird that looked a lot like the first one, except that it had white feathers sticking out of the bottom of its head instead of black ones on top.

"Uncle Foon!" chirped the yaaah-yaaah. "There's a dragon in the orchard!" And it flapped and yaaahed until it was far away and looked like one of those things that had buzzed around the tail of the creature that said, "Mmmmuuuuhh!"

Meanwhile, the white-fringed bird waddled up the hill, fastening two round pieces of ice over its eyes. "Now, now, Nephew Chung, there's no such thing as a dragon. A dragon is a mythical— Yaaah!" And it flapped and yaaahed down the hillside just as the other bird had done.

"All right, that's enough!" said Foy Rin Jin. "This place is too strange for me. And rude as well. I'm going home!" And he headed for his mountain.

But before he'd gone ten steps, he spied on the horizon a plume of black smoke curling lazily into the sky.

A DRAGON! There's another dragon down here! Foy Rin Jin gleefully galloped toward the smoke.

A few gallops later, he arrived at the scene. There were many funny-looking wooden caves, and fire was shooting out of one of them. A lot of creatures were running around, flapping and yaaahing and shouting things like "Fire!" and "Help!" and "The town hall is on fire!" but there was no sign of a dragon.

How do you make fire without a dragon?

Catching sight of Foy Rin Jin, the creatures began to screech things like "A dragon! A dragon!"— "Chung was right!"—"Stone it!"—"Cut off its head!" Then they began running around Foy Rin Jin, yaaahing and tapping him with long sticks and throwing stones, until one of the stones hit him in his delicate snout—and *hurt*!

Suddenly Foy Rin Jin knew what *mean* meant. These creatures were *peoples* and they *were* mean and they'd found a way to make a fire without a dragon and since they knew it wasn't as good as dragon fire and since a real . . . well, almost real . . . dragon had come, they were afraid he'd make a *better* fire and that was why they were trying to hurt him. Foy Rin Jin began to get REAL MAD!

Well, okay then, if it was a REAL fire they wanted . . . a REAL DRAGON fire, he'd GIVE 'em one . . . maybe . . . please . . . just this once. . . .

Foy Rin Jin lowered his great head toward the ground and began inhaling until his sides expanded and his face turned a rich purple as he spun around like a top, a tempest, a titanic tornado! Peoples clung to each other for dear life. And . . .

WHOOORRSSHHH! The universe shook—a typhoon, a tidal wave, an ocean! Then—silence. Only the hiss of steam remained, rising from where the fire had been. And the wet, wheezing whimper of a disgraced and despondent dragon. Foy Rin Jin, shamed far beyond the humiliation he had suffered at home—*let them do it!*—lifted his head slightly to offer them his snout, his eyes pleading for them to finish him quickly.

A portly little peoples came puffing through the mob and stood before him. The peoples said, "Pardon me, sir or madam. My name is Yik Moo Jong, and I am the Lord Mayor of this—*harumph!*—fair city. Would you kindly tell us your—*harumph!*—name?"

"Foy Rin Jin," whispered Foy Rin Jin. *Oh, why are they so mean?* he thought. *Why don't they get it over with?*

Then Yik Moo Jong proclaimed, "Foy Rin Jin, having saved the town hall of our—*harumph!*—fair city, is hereinafter and henceforth declared a hero, or—*harumph!*—heroine, for as long as he, she, or it may live, and is hereby granted all the rights, privileges, and titles pertaining to—*harumph!*—dragons of his, her, or its status."

The crowd chanted, "Foy! Rin! Jin! Foy! Rin! Jin!" and began to cheer and applaud, tearing off the tops of their heads and tossing them into the air.

They gave Foy Rin Jin the icehouse to live in because it was nice and cool, and they painted it red in his honor. They gave him a

fine red hat for his head and a bell to wear around his neck. And whenever there was a fire, one peoples would ride on his head and another on his tail, and he would run to the fire and try to make it a better one, a dragon fire. . . .

But it was always the same. He would spout out water everywhere, and they cheered him anyway. While it wasn't true that they were mean, they *were* a bit wacky, yelling, "Foy! Rin! Jin!" every time he failed.

Yet their cheers—and their encouragement and love—gave him a nice feeling that someday—somehow— he *would* succeed, and then, *oh!* what a glorious fire he would make for them!

"One of these days," whispered Foy Rin Jin as they cheered him on, "one of these fine days . . ."

P.S. A rumor persists that Foy Rin Jin's legendary adventures are still celebrated in today's world, that huge red thingamajigs rush to fires as he did and try vainly, as he did, to make them into bigger, better fires, and that peoples along the way still point and shout,

"Foy! Rin! Jin!"

—or something like that.

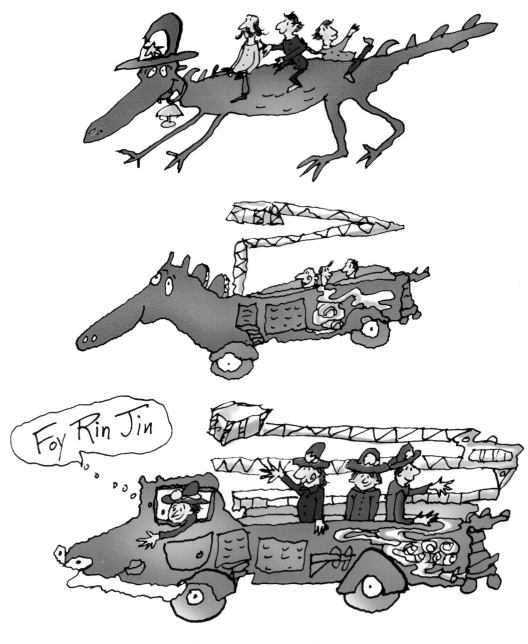

Of course, it's only a rumor. . . .